MY STORY

By

CC McBride

Copyright : CC McBride(2009)   **ISBN 978-1-4092-5715-8**

PROLOGUE

I wrote this story solely as a kind of therapy.

I had to, or else Frog would have eaten me, like the fly he thinks I am.

I hated writing it. I loved writing it. On the whole I feel better after finishing it.

Frog was right (as usual!).

While the experiences don't fill me with terror and panic anymore, I still miss the closeness of a family.

Certain names and stuff were changed, although the real names will not raise an eyebrow of recognition.

I promise I am not contravening any laws.

I have grown up I think. I do not consider myself the pivot on which the world revolve anymore.

And best of all, I do not exist at all.

Enjoy reading!

_CC_

THE START

I have never tried to write a story before…

Maybe it's high time I did. If it is just to get rid of the dark thoughts and temptations that run trough my mind, then I've accomplished something.

I grew up in the streets. The first thing I remembered of that time was my father sending me to the local KFC to beg for food. I was four years old.

I learned early to scarf some of the food before giving it to my father. He would sell it for a few pennies to the others living in our street and as soon as he had enough money, buy cheap drugs.

My parents were drug addicts.

I watched my father died of an overdose of heaven knows what. I watched my mother selling her body for just one more fix while I watched from the dumpster that was my room and bed. The last fix got her killed in a gangbang session. Not one of the men noticed that her neck was broken.

I guess I was lucky that neither of my parents thought off 'selling' me for their daily fix.

After staying with my mother until I couldn't stand the stink, I walked to the beach, a few city blocks down the way.

How clean the ocean looked! And warm, so inviting! I remember that a cool wind was blowing, telling me to play in the shallows. I can say truthfully that was the first time in my life that I laughed. Running and skipping trough the small waves, the greedy fingers of the sea tickling my feet, hard soles from never having any shoes.

That was until a bigger wave swept me of my feet, dragging me in deep. At first I tried to fight to stay afloat, not drowning. Until the cold water felt like a warm blanket and I surrendered.

…. Then somebody rudely grabbed me from that comfort, pummeled my body and screamed at me not to die! Oh! How I hated that voice!

I struggled against waking up. What did I have to live for, in any case? But the voice was very insistent. I finally opened my eyes when that person slapped me hard on my cheek.

That was how I met my new mother, Wanda Parker.

NEW BEGINNINGS

I was only ten years old when she found me.

To me she looked like an angel. Long blond hair and the bluest eyes you will never see in nature anywhere else. A small woman, and so fine it look like a small breeze can blow her away.

But she had the biggest heart in the universe, much bigger than her small body.
Ignoring my struggles and screams, she picked me up, held me close and just whispered nonsense words in my ear, all the while rocking me.

I can't remember what she said, or even my answers, if I did answer her. We walked for hours on the beach, picking up shells and polished glass and even a crab. And never did she stop talking, or laughing or sometimes just run for the fun of it.

When the sun dived towards the ocean I was so tired that I fell asleep on the warm sand.

I woke up screaming in a strange place, and a miracle! A bed! In my short life I never lived in a house, or slept in a real bed, not that I can remember anyway.

'Hey', a new voice greeted me. A little boy, not much taller than me, but dark-skinned, black wavy hair and big chocolate eyes was staring at me.

He touched my hair and face, traced the tears on my cheeks and say in the softest voice: 'You look like a dirty dolly'

'I'm not a dolly!' I screamed at him, not that I knew what a dolly was.

'Cameron, stop teasing the child! She is the prettiest doll I ever seen! And don't you say that again!'

She scolded, but with a smile on her face. Even I could see the real love for this boy in her eyes and the way she touched him on his head.

'What's your name?' Cameron asked, never taking his eyes of me.

'My name is Caren Christine McBride, and I don't have a mommy or daddy. They are dead.' Lifting my chin and blinking wildly so as not to let fresh tears flow.

'Well CC McBride! Then it is high time someone takes over! From now on, I will be your mother! Will you like that?'

In that few words, my life changed forever.

ADAPTATION

The next few weeks were pure hell.

I could not adapt. Used to being alone, fending for myself, it was cruelly strange to be hugged and kissed.

Nightmares kept on haunting me. I woke up screaming and crying the first few weeks only to find that I am in the arms of this strange being that smelled so nice and clean.

I soon learned that Cameron was also one of Ma 's pick-me-up children. To this day I don't know how many children was taken of the streets and raised by her. I know I was the last.

Cameron was barely a year older than me, but he took it on himself to look after me when Wanda was not home. At first this little boy frightened me with his dark intent look. At eleven years old he was much wiser than his years suggested.

He never called me a dirty little dolly again.
The first time he had to handle one of my dark moments he, without any outward show of emotion, put his arms around me and told me that he will chase all the boogies away.

I could not help laughing. Tears streaming down my face I screamed with laughter, holding my tummy.

After that episode I had the strength to go outside the house, inspecting my new home.

It was a small house, three bedrooms, kitchen, bathroom and living room.

And a small garden...

That was my retreat, between the rosebushes that grew any which way. The prickly coolness of the grass. The heavenly smell of roses in full bloom. I swear I can still smell it...

Just when I thought I was safe from the outer world, Ma suggested I go back to school. At first I was puzzled. School? I never went to school! Why should I go now?

Ma tried, and I tried too, as not to disappoint her. We soon learnt that I had a fear of people, especially a crowd of them in one place. I was catatonic with fear and I did not even make it to the schoolmaster's office.

She took me home.

INTERACTION

The next year Ma spent all her time home schooling me. Form 1st grade right up to grade 5. At first I couldn't understand what all the fuss was about. After all, I didn't need schooling in the past. Why now? Paper was used for other things in my past, not reading.

But then the lure of books became too hard to ignore. I had to find out what was inside those beautiful covers, what did the people in the pictures told each other? Why did this girl cry? What was so funny for this kid to laugh so hard?

It didn't took me long after that to learn to read, write and count. I used to work so hard just to get more free time to page trough Ma's extensive library.

She had something about everything, from ordinary Mills and Boon, right up to Molliere, Victor Hugo, and my favorite of favorites, Khalil Gibran – The Prophet.

To this day I can tell with conviction that the true meaning of his work went right past me. I still find it hard to understand. But I can use my imagination and that I did. I became lost in the flowery words of wisdom and wishes.

The year I turned thirteen Ma decided it was time to try a real school again. In the past years she had put her life on hold to help me and she thought it was best to meet other children of my age.

Cameron was too much of an introvert to help me cope with real life. By that time I thought of him as my brother. He would come into the room where Ma taught me and just stare at us with that sad, big brown eyes of his that was way too big for his thin frame.

Now that I think of it, I never heard him laugh out loud. It was only this small smile of his that barely lifted the corners of his mouth. But he would always be there when I needed him. When I woke up from a bad dream, he will be sitting on my bed, holding my hand.

When I cry for some reason or other, he would wipe my tears with his fingers and tell me that tears are bad for my angel eyes. He could brush my hair for hours without pulling. But when he spoke, it was only a few words, as if was afraid to speak.

I miss him so!

Ma thought it best to put me in a Catholic girls' School. With only a handful of girls, it was the best choice for me.

GUIDELINES

Even tough I never made close friends with any of the girls; I enjoyed their company. I never participated much in what they talked about but always listened avidly.

That is also where I found out what I love to do..

Cooking for one. But I was terrible at it, and still am. Surely I am the only person in the world that can burn water! I should say that my coffee is a masterpiece.

The other was needlework.

What fun! Taking a piece of material and making something wearable out of it! But the nuns did not like the way I worked. My designs and needlework did not conform to their standards.

There was a certain way they wanted things, and that is the way it should stay: no deviation.

Ma understood though. She took me shopping and we had a whale of a time! It must have cost her a small fortune to buy reams and reams of material, gauzes, ribbons, buttons, zips and heaven knows what else. The most expensive surely was the sewing machines.

I was at my happiest designing and cutting out the dresses, jackets, pants and shirts. Not that I always made a good job of it. The biggest drawback to my newfound career was the most important.

I can't draw.

The fact frustrated me no end. I have this brilliant ideas, but no way have ever committing it to paper.

So Ma called in the help of one of her friends..

REVELATIONS

Ok, I know. I should have suspected that a beautiful woman like Ma would have friends. And a lot of them. I found out things about her after her death that could have been left unsaid.

Maybe I will write about that later.

Ma knew Nick for years. I fell madly in love with him the first time I saw him. Over 2 meters long, broad shoulders, leanly muscled and the most unruly blonde hair that was his secret despair.

I was shyly hiding behind Ma when he arrived. He kneeled until he was face level with me and said in his deep soft voice:

'Who is this pretty little lady, Wanda?'

He loosened my hand that was gripping Ma's dress and kissed my fingers. I was immediately smitten.

'My name is Caren Christine McBride.' I said proudly, although I tried to hide the fear I still felt after all the years that past.

Of course I saw men in the streets! But I was always looking at their eyes, waiting for a sign that they planned to attack or something. My past still haunts me to this day.

But he was Ma 's friend. I was sure I could trust him.

He knew people who knew people who knew what to do when a girl wants to design and can't draw. They designed a program that can change my scribbling into what I had in mind.

With newfound freedom I scribbled on the pad with a 'pen' and where I wanted a straight line, a straight line I would get. Every conceivable angle was thought of. I had a blast!

At first I made clothes for Ma and Cameron. That was the start. They never wore any other clothes until the day they died.
When I turned fourteen I was home again. Doing my senior schooling on the computer at Ma 's insistence. The rest of my time I made clothes.

And I turned Goth..

HIDING

When people remarked on the clothes Ma wore, and that of me and Cameron, Ma very proudly would inform them that her daughter designed and made it herself. Then the selfsame people would look at me, not with surprise, but with pity.

They did not have to say anything. I knew exactly what they thought. My suspicions were proven right when I overheard one old biddy berating Ma for allowing me to work for a living.

Ma was livid with anger. The first time that I saw her like that. And it scared me.

Let me try to explain:

Ma was small. Really small. Thin and short. She barely reached the 1.6-meter mark with her high heels. But her love for her children made her look enormous. So did her wrath.

We never saw that woman again. She was big and fat, and she let Ma scare her away.
It was not long after that that some of Cameron's schoolmates asked me to make something for them too.

Cameron had this one peculiarity: he loved leather. When I made him his first jacket, he demanded leather pants to go with it. And a waistcoat. Expensive. But he was my brother and I indulged him.

He very proudly wore those clothes with an air of distinction.

And the boys wanted what Cameron had.

Ma insisted that I sell the clothes with a hefty profit. They wanted it, after all..

And soon the boys' girlfriends came with them. I tried to make friends with them, comfortable in my new life. But I was beneath their notice. I had to listen to their snide remarks of a dumb blonde, good for nothing, boyfriend stealer. Nothing that Ma said could take a way the hurt.

So. I turned Goth.

Dyed my hair black. Black make-up. Black clothes. Long dresses or pants with long shirts to hide my body. I became unsmiling and rude.

The boys soon learned that a bad attitude from their girlfriends would not get them the clothes they so desired. They had a choice, and most of them chose to wear my clothes.

INDEPENDENCE

Ma was not happy with my change. But she understood and let me be. She said that she knew her sweet CC was underneath all the gunk I put on my face.

Not yet a full fourteen years old, my 'business' became too large for Ma's little house. And all the children demanding I made something for them were beginning to irritate her.

So, like only Wanda Parker can be, she made a plan.

Let me first explain something:

Ma was not rich. She worked for a living. After her children went to bed, she would sit up for hours, doing bookkeeping for small firms. She didn't get much sleep, I think.

With the help of her friend, Nick, she found this little apartment nearly right on the beachfront. It was an ideal workplace for me.

And right across the street from the building, a mere ten paces away, was the flea market.

One morning when I woke up, all my materials and machines were gone. Before I could have panicked, Ma came in the room with a smile on her face that told me she had something to do with the disappearance of my things.

'I have a surprise for you, little girl,' she said, even though I was taller than her at that stage. She was jumping all over the place from excitement. For the first time she didn't care about my lessons, she just wanted to show me my surprise.

The apartment was perfect.

Shelves covered the one wall in the living room. A big cutting table in the middle, nearly dwarfing the already small room. My machines lined up in front of the window that opens on a small balcony.

There was also a small kitchen, a bedroom with its own bathroom. All fully stocked.

Ma arranged all my stuff just the way I liked it: everything in its place, and in easy reach.

I couldn't say anything; I just fell into her arms and cried. I had all a girl can dream to have: except one thing.

MAKING FRIENDS

So. Every day after my stint at schooling, I would take the bus to my new.. Yes. I will call it that, my studio!

I couldn't wait.

To not disappoint Ma, I swot like a crazy person, getting top marks in all my subjects.

It took me only fourteen months to complete Grade 10 to Grade 12. Although Ma never pushed me to do anything other than to follow my dreams, I could see that she was proud of me.

Her hugs and kisses could convey a world of feelings that her words cannot express.

Then Uncle Nick decided that it was time to introduce me to society.

At first I was heavily against the idea, but Ma insisted. She told me I couldn't expect my clothes to sell only by word of mouth; I have to 'network'. Wear one of my dresses and impress the city, make myself known.

Uncle Nick promised it would not be a big occasion, only a select few. Knowing him, I didn't quite believe him. And sure enough, for a young girl not yet seventeen, the few hundred people was a crowd, and I panicked.

I ran.

But before I even reached the doors, Uncle Nick grabbed me, and absolutely no-care for my dress, hoisted me on one shoulder and marched laughingly right into the center of the crowd.

Now, I already told how big Uncle Nick was. He was already head and shoulders above most of his guests. And with me on his shoulder, I was the center of attention.

That accentuated another problem of mine; with my fair skin, I blush easy. This time was no exception. I was redder than a fire hydrant, and the color of my face clashed horribly with my dress.

But it worked like magic. Soon I had so many orders for clothes, ranging from ball dresses to one-of-a-kind jeans, I knew I would be busy for the next few months. In my mind I was already choosing colors and styles for the women.

With Ma as my bookkeeper, I didn't have a care in the world.

NICHOLAS WILLCOTT

Uncle Nick was a lawyer and friends with Ma for years. I couldn't get enough of his story of how he met Ma.

He just finished his law studies and was due to start work at a law firm the next month. Driving home from a visit to his parents, he saw something that nearly caused an accident.

A ramshackle VW Beetle was pulled of the highway and it was clear from the distance that the vehicle had a flat tyre.

But it was not the car that had drawn his attention; it was of the owner, doing a handstand on the roof of the car.

Now all of us know that a VW Beetle has a round shape and at time, the body was made of metal, not plastic or whatever they make cars of now.

He pulled his car over, watching this teenager as he first thought, doing a handstand, and occasionally a back flip to her feet, and then back on her hands again. When she nearly slipped of the roof he decided it was time to intervene.

Now, Uncle Nick was a BIG man, and I mean, really BIG! But he moved as silently as a cat. No stone crunch under his feet, it was as if his feet never touched the ground.

It was when Ma made one of her back flips, that he caught her in mid-air, placing her on solid ground. And got paid for his trouble where men don't liked to be kicked. He fell to ground, clutching his pained body-parts, groaning like a dying man.

She left him there until the pain subsided, never saying a word. When he looked up from his position on the ground, it was to find her with a tyre-lever in her hands, ready to strike.

'Lady, if this is the way you repay a person who is trying to help, then no wonder you are still beside the road!'

Ma laughed then, and held out her hand. 'I am Wanda Parker, and who may you be?'

That was when, he told me, and he fell in love with her. His fairy-girl.

But Ma had no time for lovers; she was enjoying her life too much. Falling in love was easy, she said, it was staying in love that was hard work.

For that, there was no time in her life.

WANDA PARKER AND CAMERON

That was her name. An angel God sent to help the babies on earth.

There were several homeless kids on the streets, hundreds, if not thousands. I will never know the real reason why she picked just a few of us.

Cameron was her first one. She loved to tell us how she was out shopping for a suitable pair of shoes when the sound of a little kitten drew her attention.

She followed the sound into an alley filled with refuse bags and without thought to her clean clothes and manicured nails, she rummaged through it.

What she found was not a kitten like she first thought, but a newborn baby, dirty, with the umbilical cord still attached and bleeding.

She didn't think much of her bright yellow jacket when she took it off and wrapped him up and took him to the nearest hospital.

He checked out fine. Just very hungry and a little bit angry. Ma fed the little baby with the bottles the hospital provided.

Ma couldn't leave him alone. The police couldn't find his birth mother or any one that knows of a girl who gave birth on that day. She could not let him disappear in the Welfare system.

So she called in the help of her friend, Nicholas Willcott. He was a highly respected lawyer and pulled some strings. A few months later Ma adopted Cameron Nicholson. The irony of Cameron's name only became apparent after the tragedy that took Ma's life.

Wanda Parker, lovingly called 'Wawa' by her family, became a mother at the age of 20 to a little boy that was thrown in the rubbish by his birth mother.

Her friends called her crazy. Most of them never spoke to her again. The few that stayed supported her and together they raised Cameron.

Nick was one that stayed. He doted on Cameron. Ironically Ma said that he was acting like a real father to the baby.

Cameron had a carefree happy childhood, until he went to school for the first time and one of the children called him a rubbish because he was picked out of a refuse heap.

He was devastated. Ma told him the truth. That was the end of his happiness. He became silent and never laughed again.

CAMERON AGAIN…

Although he became silent and withdrawn, he took me under his wing. In the beginning he was never far from me, filling in for Ma when she was of doing her business.

He never asked anything from anybody, preferring to earn his way. When he was not busy with school or me, he worked for Uncle Nick.

Too young to understand that legally, the 'work' he done was just Uncle Nicks' way of keeping him happy. Paying him a small steady sum every month made Cameron feel that he was worth something.

He started by pulling out weeds, and then steadily graduated to more responsible jobs.

Like cutting the grass. The day when the head landscaper decided that Cameron could prune the roses was a milestone in his life.

When he turned sixteen, Ma bought him his first dirt bike. Soon enough he had his license and went tearing of into the veldt. More than once he came home with a scrape or a tear.

That was also the time that he asked Uncle Nick to search for his parents. For Ma it was a shock. If the police couldn't find a trace of his parents, why would Nick be able to?

But Uncle Nick had access to resources that Ma can only dream of. Who knew that he was leading a double life? And he did find Cameron's' real family. Unfortunately, it also took Cameron away from us.

The ink wasn't yet dry on his last senior exam when he packed up his clothes and left us. With promises to come back regularly, which he did.

But nothing was the same after that.

I missed him. I could see that Ma was a little bit lost without him in the house. But she never denied him his family. After all, why would he stay in a small house in a big city, when he had grandparents on a farm that he would one day inherit? Although they never found their daughter, her son would perpetuate the family name.

Cameron was as happy as he could be. But he never found the peace in his soul that he craved.

CHANGES

Things changed a lot after he left us. To tell the truth, we saw more of Cameron than we did before.

Where he always hid in his bedroom, or later taking his bike out for a spin, he now sat down with us, talking.

He had a lot to talk about. About his new family, how the family doctor insisted on DNA tests to make sure that Cameron was part of the family.
He didn't care about that. He had this whole piece of earth where he can hide in plain sight. The farm became his passion.

When his grandparents died in a car accident a few months later, Cameron divided the cattle and few goats between the farm workers, deeding them a piece of the farm.

He renovated the old homestead and built a lookout tower, where he would sit most nights, watching the stars trough a telescope.

Not that he was rich by any standards, but he could live comfortably out of the trust that his grandparents made in his name.

He pretty much could do what he wanted. But he chose to spend his time between the farm and us.

But things were never the same between Ma and Nick. Let me drop the pose; he never was and never will be my uncle, in hindsight he doesn't deserve my respect.

I could see that Ma was struggling to come to terms with the loss of Cameron and Nick being the author of that loss.

Six months after I finished my senior exams, Ma presented me with the deed of the apartment as a birthday present.

I just turned seventeen.

I am not the scared little girl bent on self-destruction she found years ago.

I had my own business, being quite successful.

I decided it was time to move on.

Ma was 38 years old.

MORE CHANGES…

The first few nights alone in my new apartment was terrible. I had trouble sleeping and when I did fell asleep, the smallest sound would wake me.

Then I usually got up and start designing, cutting patterns, sewing and finishing whatever project or order I had.

It was one of those nights that a soft knock at the door interrupted my concentration.

Being careful like Ma urged me to be, I first checked through the spy-hole.

It was my new neighbor, aunt Gertie. We met when I dragged my suitcases up the stairs because the elevator was broken, again.

This time when opened the door, she had a little present for me, a little kitten. A gray Persian with blue eyes.

By the time I had made aunt Gertie some coffee, the kitten was fast asleep on my most expensive material. Deep red velvet. That was when I decided to call her Queenie.

Aunt Gertie and Queenie became fixtures in my life. Like Ma.

Queenie was happy as long as she had her food and some milk and a sandbox in the corner of my room. Not that she ever used it much. Even though I am living on the fourth floor, Queenie found a way out and down.

More than once I had to open my front door to her insistent scratching and would without a by your leave, curl up on the pillow I made of the velvet.

Aunt Gertie got in the habit of making me dinner after she witnessed my sorry excuse for trying to fix her something to eat one night. As payment I would make her something, a dress or two, a few blouses, skirts and even once a coat, my first try.

She loved the coat.

Ma would visit during the day, mostly just sitting watching me and sipping coffee.

Then one day, she dropped a bomb on me.

'I am in love.' She told me calmly. But the absolute pure love in her eyes belied her calmness. She was serious. 38 years old, and fully in love for the first time in her life. I wonder what Nick would say about it.

MA IN LOVE?

Ma loved everyone.

I mean; there is not one person in this world that could hate Ma. She was too happy and treated every person she met with grace and respect. She never treated any one with different than the others. Albeit the beggar on the street, or one of her highflying social light grabbing acquaintances.

Ma had crowds of friends of which I only met a few and remembers none. The only constant friend in her life was Nick. But even Nick was persona non grata on New Years' Eve.

I found out later what she and her friends were up to at that time; but that subject is not up for discussion.

I remember the disaster when a one-time boyfriend named Oliver moved in with us when I was thirteen. In hindsight I know that she did not loved him.

My point is: Ma loved many, but never truly fell in love with a man. Never!

Until she told me that she loved, deeply. That was a real shock to me.

'I want you to meet him.' She told me casually.

Another shock.

'Ma!'

'Oh yes! I told him about you and he wants to meet my little girl.' She smiled happily. I could see that the constraints of keeping the news quiet was finally broken. She wiggled about and could not sit still, as if she had a problem containing her happiness.

She looked at her watch.

'In the next five minutes! You don't mind me using your computer, do you?' not waiting for an answer, she saved my work, connected her cell on my computer, and logged on.

She connected YM and activated my web cam.

'Hey Love! Do you want to meet my daughter?'

I watched the picture on the small screen. My night of shocks was not over.

18

THE STRANGER

I had everything I needed.

I had a thriving business, my own space, loving family and good friends.

There was just this one thing that was missing. All these years I thought it was just dreams.

Since my twelve birthday, not long after I had my first, well, first sign that I was leaving my childhood behind, I had this dream.

A very lucid dream. I did not feel like I was dreaming.

I dreamt it was winter. Very cold. But I was enjoying the cold wind and light snow against my face.

I was sitting in front of a wooden house, not a log cabin, but a house built of solid wooden slabs and stone. I remember the house clearly. One day I will build that house.

The snow was deep. A few treetops were visible in the distance, but the snow was cleared around the house.

A man and a little girl were playing in the snow. The little blonde girl was chasing the man and he was letting her catch him, with protestations of how fast she was and how old he was, to show him some mercy.

Then he would pick her up, turn to me and wave at me. The little girl screamed and laughed and pulls at the man's ears. Then she would throw me little kisses with her mittened hands.

It was clear in my dream that the girl was my daughter, and the man my husband. That we lived high in the mountains in a beautiful house. We are living well. But they were talking in a strange language, which in my dreams I understood.

I never understood why I never joined them in their play.

Now I know why.

The man Ma fell in love with, was the man in my dreams.

I ran.

BITTER TRUTH

As always, Ma knew exactly where to find me.

By the ocean like she did all those years ago. Like then, I was in no mood to talk to her.

If anyone asked me if I hated, if would have answered no. I never did. Even with my real parents I was too small to understand what was going on. But I am not that little girl anymore.

I told her about my dream after the first few times. She told me I was dreaming of my future, and not to disregard it. I took her at her word and built my life around that dream.

She knew exactly who that man was. And still she took him for herself.

Why didn't she leave me to drown all those years ago?

Rage was boiling in my body. It made me feel powerful, about to burst. I lashed out. I dragged out all the bad words I remembered from the streets, screaming it to her face. I hit her wherever I could.

And she let me. Standing still taking all that I dished out.

Until I became tired, sank to my knees crying. Huge raw sounds tearing from my body. I felt helpless, hopeless. What chance did I have against her? What man would prefer me before her?

I lost my dream.

'He doesn't like your hair black.'

Ma's voice, soft and full of sympathy, reached me. 'Please understand, CC. I will have him to myself only for a little while; you will have him for the rest of your life. Won't you give me that?'

I didn't care. I got up and left her standing there.

Things were never the same between us after that. I took to traveling, leaving Queenie with Aunt Gertie. When I touched home base, I preferred to stay with Nick. Using my apartment only as a work place.

But I did go back to my natural hair color.

MAKING A NAME

The next few months I was out to show the world what I was made of. Even though I was blonde again, I retained my rude and abrupt manner.

I visited fashion houses, attended shows, even once in a while presented a few designs myself.

Hote couture hated me, but the public went crazy over my clothes. I designed specifically with teenagers in mind, splashing out on more formal designs when the urge struck me.

I was being noticed.

My biggest drawback was the fact that I never studied in designing. I was always invited to show a outfit or two, but was always cut out of the sifting for talent because I was too young, I was too market specific, blah blah!

I did not care.

I was making money and I loved it!

That was also the time that I took up paragliding with a vengeance. The total freedom I experienced in the air made me forget everything. I forgot that reality exists. It was just the wind and I.

I always landed with a run, slide and a bump. Right on my hiney. That quick, sometimes painful landing would shake me into reality. But I tasted freedom for a few hours, or less and at that time it was enough to clear my head a bit.

I also procured a stall in the flea market right over the street from my apartment and was welcomed by the other hawkers like family.

Every morning I would get up early, pack the clothes I finished the night and opened the stall. I rarely slept more than a few hours, preferring to create rather than being chased by bad dreams.

I never remembered my dreams, except THE one. But where it previously made me happy, it turned sour.
Like Ma said, I am young, I will soon find another man more suitable to my age.

Men? Who cares? Not me! Let Ma waste her time with that man, I would much rather forget about him.

Anyway, I was far too busy doing what I love.

JAMES

The trip from Nick's house to the city was beginning to tell on me. I soon began sleeping at my apartment again. I missed that big old house of his. Built in the late 1800s, it boasted a mix of architectural structures, from the more formal to the bizarre.

It had an enormous garden, a heated pool of Olympic proportions and a Jacuzzi. My favorite of course was the rose gardens. At night I would open my window wide and fell asleep with the smell of roses in my nose.

It was a letdown sleeping in a city that is never quiet. I worked myself to stupefaction, most of the times just sleeping where I worked.

One morning, struggling with the load of clothes I finished the night before, a stranger asked me if he could help me carry the bags.

I knew his face. He lived in my building, a floor down. I noticed him a few times, watching me.

'My name is James,' holding out his right hand. I swear, sometimes I hated the fact that I was so.. white, but right then I was glad I was not a redhead. The poor man blushed under his freckles right up to his ears.

I giggled. I couldn't help it. It was really funny! Here was this tall, thin man, most probably hating the fact of his coloring, folding his hand, yeah, fold! around mine.

I was sure that we were looking quite ridiculous. Like characters out of some spoof movie. He was tall, thin and red, and I small, a little bit round and blonde. We were both the color of my best velvet.

That was the start of our friendship. Every morning he would help me with my bags and at night he would walk with me to the bank to deposit my takings for the day.

He was 23 years old and a student in architecture, working part time at a local firm to finance his studies.

Even though I enjoyed his company, it was not long before the travel bug bit me again.

This time, the committee from the biggest show in South Africa sent me an invitation to show a collection of my clothes.

I grabbed at the chance. The fact that I didn't see Ma for a couple of months did not bother me one bit.

THE ATTACK

A week before my show, running around, changing and changing again the clothes I wanted to show, I got a call from Cameron.

I immediately felt a sense of dread. Cameron never calls, he always just showed up. Why he ever invested in a cell phone was beyond my ken.

When he spoke, I could hear the fear in his voice.

'Ma was attacked this morning. Zeus and Freia are dead. She is in hospital. Come home.'

The phone went dead.

I left everything. Just like that. I just grabbed my bag, jumped in my car, and swore at the 1.200 kilometers that was lying between Ma and me.

How I made the trip without causing an accident was beyond me. I stopped twice to fill up my tank, grabbing a burger and coke, eating when I can. I tried calling Cameron repeatedly, but he was on voicemail. Even Nick was out of contact. His secretary Tom Middleton couldn't or wouldn't tell me where he was.

To this day I don't know why I went straight for that specific hospital. There are several hospitals, but I went straight to the one where Ma was. I didn't even pause in the lobby, taking the stairs, my senses leading me straight to Ma. Right by her door I was stopped by two men. Later it would sink in. Thankful for being small and young, I slid in the room between them before they could grab me.

The big body of Nick hid the bed. In the corner of the room Cameron was leaning against the wall. Ignoring both, I jumped on the bed.

'Ma! Don't die!' I screamed, the terror only then taking hold of me.

She looked terrible, but tried to laugh.

'I am not dying little girl. I am just a little banged up, is all.'

Then she started crying.

'They killed my dogs!'

She didn't seem able to stop crying. I could see that every sob hurt her badly, but she was unable to stop. A nurse scurried in and gave her an injection. The terrible sound stopped when Ma fell asleep.

IF..

Even in her sleep the terror of her ordeal was still etched on her face. The part of her face that was not covered with a bandage was discolored and swollen.

I turned on Cameron.
'What happened?' he just stared at me, no expression on his face. But he was taking it hard; I can see that in his eyes. He also had no plan on answering me.

'Nick?' realizing too late that I forgot to address him as 'uncle'.

He has changed. The once happy smiling face was etched in lines and his eyes were red and puffy, as if he was crying.

Taking a deep breath, stropping his hands over his face in frustration, he nearly yelled: 'I don't know! I found her this morning, lying under Freia. I thought she was dead!

There was so much blood!'

He paced the small room angrily.

'Zeus was shot in the head. Freia was stabbed. Wanda was lying under her. The dog nearly crushed her!'

I couldn't get anything out of him that made sense. Apparently two colored men attacked Ma, one with the gun, and the other with a knife.

Ma always had a hard time sleeping, but this time she had someone to keep her company. The foreigner. She was without sleep for 36 hours. She did not arm the alarm at all that night.

At five o' clock the morning the dogs started barking. She got up and was in time to see Zeus got shot. Freia tried to protect Ma, jumping at the man with the knife that was waiting for Ma. The dog ripped the man's throat out, but not before he cut and stabbed Ma. Freia paid with her life for her loyalty.

I saw the intense hatred in Nick's eyes when he spoke of that man, which I shared wholeheartedly at that moment.

If he didn't keep Ma awake that night, she would have checked that her gate was locked, that her alarm system was activated. She would have remembered to take her gun with her when the dogs barked.

If.. if..

DOUBLE LIFE

Ma's attack revealed the truth about Nick.

Don't get me wrong! He loved Ma with a passion. But it was also a clinging overly protective jealous love.

In his rage he revealed things that shocked me to the bone. At that time he was still my hero, but the more he ranted, the colder I felt in my soul.

He ruled her life. He had her followed everywhere. She did not speak to one person that he did not know of. She only had friends HE approved of. Every person that set foot in her house was thoroughly checked.

The people he did not approve of, he bought of, and if that did not work, he got rid of them. My mind refused to think of how.

Nick was rich. Very rich. Money was not important to him except as a tool to get what he wanted. He wanted it all. And that included Ma.

'I will kill him!' he stated with conviction.

I had no doubt that he would have, but Ma kept the foreigners' whereabouts to herself.

Only I knew where he was, and that only the country.

Later I would find out that Nick spent a fortune trying to find that man. Nick did not like losing. He was losing this battle. He knew Ma loved this man and he had no way of getting rid of him. Ma was not totally blind to what Nick really was then.

One thing of Ma, she loved to surf the Internet. She would put a word in Google search just to see what the results would be. One of this random searches brought up this trivia site, and she joined immediately. In a foreign language but with English questions.

One her first day there, answering questions that was common knowledge to her, this man spoke to her. They became friends. He just lost a dear friend and he spoke to Ma about it. Typically, Ma offered her sympathy.

They spoke on Yahoo. Later with the web cam, but at that time Ma was already in love with him.

When Ma couldn't accompany Nick to functions she usually attended with him, he wondered why. He found out soon enough. He knew he was losing her, and for him, that was not an option.

SECRETS REVEALED

Nick had a wonderful family. His parents and a brother. That his name was different from his family, never raised a question in my mind.

His father was owner and CEO of a brick manufacturing business and quite successful. But that was not where Nick got his money from.

He was the apple of his grandmothers' eye, and when she died, he inherited all her assets. Included was the house he lived in.

It still is a beautiful house. Situated in a few acres, it ensured his privacy. High walls and an electronic gate kept curious eyes out. The guard at the gate kept everyone else outside the gates, except if your name was on his list.

In hindsight the household was run like the military. There was a schedule for every minute of the day. The only people that could come and go like they pleased, was Wanda Parker and her children. The rest was by invitation only. That included his parents.

Nick's secretary was a man named Tom Middleton, a widower. His daughter Trixeille, became the cook of the household. Oh lordy! And can she cook! But she never could bake a cake. Pastries and pies and all that kind of deserts, but not cake.

She was beautiful. Long black hair right up to her hiney. Straight and glossy. She had a natural beauty that had no need for make-up. Her mother was French. She died during Trix's birth due to unknown complications.

Her father, Tom, ruled her with an iron hand. His word was law. He was a cold, bitter man. To look him in the eye was an unnerving feeling.

Nick's secretary. Yeah right!

Tom was the person that saw to it that every wish or command of Nick was obeyed.

Nick laughingly told us once about a dog that attacked Tom. With the dog still hanging with his teeth on Tom's arm, he calmly broke the neck of the dog, without flinching, without showing a glimmer of pain.

I know I am rambling a bit. I know that my sentences and words are jumbled.

But think about this: I was a friend of assassins. People that were hired to kill. And killed they did. Nick and Tom reveled in taking lives.

And Ma knew about it.

LIVING WITH FEAR

A week after Ma's attack, she insisted on leaving the hospital. Nick refused to allow her to leave.

It was only after their heated discussing that I finally really looked at Ma's face. I saw the fear in her eyes.

I sat on her bed and took her hand in mine.

'Tell me. I am big enough. I can handle the truth.'

Prophetic words. I found out that I was nothing more than a silly girl playing to be grown-up. I failed miserably.

Ma burst into tears. Huge racking sobs, like her heart was breaking. I am sure that it did. At first I had trouble understanding what she told me.

But I chained her words together. The more she told me of Nick, the more I realized the fear she was living with the past fifteen years since she met him.

Nick did not approve of her mother and brother, so he bought them of, never to visit or see her again. Of one dear friend she had from her schooldays, suddenly committing suicide, of Nick's silent rage when Ma had done something he did not approve of.

Of the disappearance of Oliver, the one man that she thought could make her happy. How one night he went outside to smoke a cigarette, and never returned. He is still on the missing persons list.

Ma feared Nick. She knew what he was, who he work for in reality, what laid behind the mask of successful lawyer and chairman of several charities.

So I called Cameron and we made a plan.

We will spirit Ma away. Nick would not find her. Never!

I looked around the country for a suitable house and found it. Not far from Cameron's farm.

A girl not yet fourteen, who recently lost her mother to brain cancer. She was selling the house to live with her grandmother in another province.

We were so naïve, thinking that Nick would not find us.

He did.

GAME, SET AND MATCH

Strange how fate takes a hand in our lives sometimes.

Danica's mother died just before Christmas. She was her mother's only child. Young, but so mature, I felt like a silly girl next to her.

Blonde, blue-eyed, long and slender with a poise that belied her years.

It turned out that her mother was a sensei in martial arts, and taught Danica from a very young age how to fight, or how not to. I am not quite sure. Tae kendo? Still not sure.

She may have looked fragile but she had a strength that few men could equal. And fast!

Cameron committed the sin of touching her once and found himself on his stomach on the floor, his arms twisted behind his back, her small foot planted between his shoulder blades.

No matter how hard he struggled, he couldn't get out of her grip. She was holding him down effortlessly.

She was fast! I was looking at her at that moment and I did not see her move!

'Never creep up to me ever again! You hear me?' Her voice was soft, but the intent was clear. Next time she will hurt him but good!

Cameron heeded the intent. But my poor brother was lost. He fell in love with this teenage ninja girl.

Ma saw that. Not long after that she spoke to Cameron, told him the girl is too young, that he should leave her alone. I thought that Ma was wrong. I knew Cameron, and he would never be anything but honorable with Danica.

Ma was not so sure. Maybe she knew things that I did not.

But besides that, I did not think that she would let some one touch her without her prior consent.

And I was right. Not long after the incident Danica told me of her mothers' life and the incentive to make sure that the girl can defend herself in any giving situation. That she did not have time for boys: her studies came first.

I thought of all the girls in Cameron's wake. Good! Let him feel the pain of unrequited love! My poor brother! But I could not help laughing at him.

CO-INCIDENCES

We were there a week, getting settled in our new home, when Danica dropped the bomb.

Her mother was 'the dear friend' that this... man, had lost.

I could see that the news shocked Ma. Her smile had become a little strained.

That night she had a fight with him. Dragged the truth from him. It turned out that Ma sent him money, which she could ill afford.

Why would a man ask money from a woman? Why would he ACCEPT money from a woman? What type of man was he?

The idea made me sick. My dream man, stolen from me by Ma, was nothing more than a gigolo, taking their money, making empty promises. How did Ma ever fell for him? How did I ever think about it?

It was at that moment that I decided that I would live my life my way, without a man.

After Danica left the town for her grandmother's, life became a bit more settled. Ma was getting better, but still plagued with nightmares of the attack. The things she found out about her 'lover' hurt her badly. By that time I was also a regular visitor on that site, making sure that Ma did not know about it.

It was not long before Reanu made his pass at me. I thought, what a nice way of getting my revenge on him! I will make him pay, for hurting me, Ma and Danica's mother. I pretended to be too young, and he fell for it. Turning into a father figure for me.

What a laugh!

Before I could do anything other than being friendly with him, our sense of freedom was shattered.

Two cars and an ambulance stopped in the driveway.

Nick and Tom Middleton were in the first car.

Four other men were in the other car and I remember thinking; oh dear God, he had to bring the local Mafia!

It was laughable how Nick thought that it was necessary to bring five men with him to take Ma back to the city.

REALITY CHECK

What I did not expect was seeing James with them.

He couldn't look me in the eye. Blushing like a teenage schoolgirl, chuffing his shoes in the ground. I slapped him as hard as I could and had the pleasure of seeing my finger marks on his face.

Nick laughed at him.

'Damn boy! Will you let a puissant girl slap you like that? This is what you are supposed to do!'

I didn't see it coming. I remember feeling a sudden pain in my face and waking up with a searing pain in my face and a thundering headache. He broke my nose and my cheekbone. He also relieved my mouth of half a tooth.

When I tried to touch my face to access the damage, I found that I was tied up.

With it came the realization that Ma was gone.

I lost it then. I screamed.

Cameron found me the next day, still screaming, but no sound coming from my mouth.

I lost my voice. My nose grew on crooked. The broken cheekbone healed with a little dent in it. I still have the scars where the ropes cut into my wrists. My voice still hoarse to this day.

Cameron tried his best to look after me. He tried to let a doctor look at me but every time someone came near me, I'd go mad.

I did recover eventually.

But I was too late to stop Ma from marrying Nick.

A month later she was dead.

I lost my mind.

I was not Caren Christine McBride anymore.

Thank God for Cameron.

RECOVERING

Cameron used that time to get me in the hospital. The doctors reset my nose and wired my broken cheekbone and jaw.

Doped up, I have no recollection of that few weeks in the hospital.

When I did finally recover my senses, I was on top of my mountain. Except for the sound of the fountain bubbling nearby, it was peacefully quiet.

My body hurt from laying still so long. I tried to move my head but stopped when excruciating pains shot trough my head.

'Don't try to move too fast, Sis. Relax. You are safe.'

Cameron's calm words brought back the reality with a bang. Unwanted memories screamed trough my mind.

'Shush, it's alright, I'm here, cry if you want to.'

He gathered me in his arms and rocked me like a baby while I wept, wetting his shirt.

Somewhere along the way I fell asleep again. When I woke up again, it was with the welcoming smell of brewing coffee scenting the night air.

Cameron refused to take me back to the city, saying that I needed time. He was right. At that moment I had hatred in my heart. I would have attacked Nick, and most probably, paid with my life for that.

I recovered slowly, the pain getting less by the day, my anger building.

One way or the other, Nicholas Willcott will pay for what he did. I don't know how, but he will.

Cameron tried to distract me from my plans. His efforts were fruitless.

Six weeks after Ma's funeral, we returned to the city.
The trek down the mountain took us five hours to complete where it usually only took me thirty minutes. That is, when I am climbing.

With flying, it took me that much longer with good currents.

When I opened my apartment door, I was met with total chaos.

INTERLUDE

It has been a few months since I wrote. But being happy do that to people I think..

And I was far HAPPIER at being happy, than I was thinking about the horrors, even if it was doctors' orders.

What girl wants to think about hate and madness when love is knocking at her door?

Not me, for sure!

Having met Steven changed my live. Well, he caught me in a good moment. Let me tell you how we met.

I was in a stage of my life where I was considering ending it all. Life was not worth living, at that time.

I had everything planned out, of how I was going to do it. But one thing... I just didn't want to be ALONE, when doing it.

So, I surfed. The Internet. Google was my starting point. I would take my dictionary, let it fall open, and just stick my finger on a word.

PIMP...

Well, I googled.

Had a few hundred, no, thousands of pages, ranging from the factual, to games.
I tried the games, never having done that before. I had my playstation, although it was a bit dusty after all these months.

I clicked on a random page, and at a random site. Came up with keeppimpin, registered, and started playing.

I SUCKED!! To put it lightly.

The irony of playing that game struck me much later.

Me, a strict Catholic, a virgin to boot, playing a whore game??

What's the odds in that?

To make my story short, I noticed the chat link on the home page. Feeling doubtful, having had some very bad experiences with chat rooms before, I clicked.

I felt a lot of trepidation, having noticed that it was an AMERICAN site.

See, I discovered that no one person is very honest on any site, any chat room. Why people have to pretend that they are something else than they really are, is above my ken.

And what I know of Americans, is what I see on TV. Not very encouraging. In my mind they were a pretentious nation, not even trying to be better than their past. Thinking that they can just carry on, that they are untouchable.

I was pleasantly surprised. More about this, much later..

First, let me get this bad stuff out of the way. Get it out of my head, so I can move on with my life, whatever the future may hold.

LOSS OF INNOCENCE

I had to fight the urge to run..

Instead I stood my ground and inspected the damage..

It was horrible.

Fabrics were torn and stained. My shelves littered the floor in pieces. Expensive sewing machines destroyed. Buttons, zippers, needles, pins, yarn, the crochet and beadwork were unrecognizable. Someone made a good job of destroying my work. And my life.

My crockery broken shards on the kitchen floor. Sugar, coffee, every packet, can or sachet of food and commodities strewn on the floor. Everything unusable.

I was devastated. I was shaking, my body ice-cold. Dreadful fear was taking over. The urge to run was overwhelming.

Cameron was tense and unsmiling, his grip painful on my arm. The pain brought a little sense back to me, he was trying to drag me out of the apartment. I was frozen on the spot.

'Caren, lets GO!'

'I need to find Queenie, I can't leave her here!'

Scrambling around through the debris that was once my existence, I called her. Stepping over broken parts, wood pieces and fabrics stained with red paint, I searched everywhere.

Then I opened my fridge door.

That was then that Cameron grabbed me and dragged me out.

Thinking back on it, I still feel the horror.

My cat, dead, frozen stiff between mangled remains of food. She had a fierce will to live.

I cannot think of it, without having nightmares. My mind still screams. Her fur matted, eyes glassy, broken nails, foamy blood frozen in her open screaming mouth.

She died horribly.

RUNNING

I do not remember much after that.

Thinking back, I acted like a total ninny, a wimp, not like someone who has been earning a living since fourteen years old.

I thought I had escaped the violent vileness of the back streets. My brain was incapable to comprehend that people with all the money in the world, all the privileges, can still act like uncivilized brutes.

I have witnessed violent fights, even a knife killing in my childhood years. Even then there was a purpose to the violence.

But….

Killing a CAT?? Stuffing it into a freezer to freeze to death?? WHY??

At one stage Cameron must have sense something was wrong, because he pulled over, grabbed me by the arms and shook me violently, slapping me when it didn't help.

That cleared my head and for the first time I noticed under what strain my brother was.

He was as white as a sheet, his teeth clenched, but with a bitter determination in his eyes. At that moment he reminded me of Nick, even though Cameron was more swarthy, the total opposite if Nicks' looks.

He pinched my nose painfully, giving my shoulder a quick squeeze when tears spilled over my cheeks.

'Caren, FOCUS!'

His voice sounded unused, a bit gravelly. I took a few deep breaths, clearing my mind, pushing the ugly images to my subconscious.

By implication I knew he was right. We have to focus, to find a way away from the madness behind us, and find a safe place for both of us.

We do not have a lot of options. No matter where we go, Nick was sure to find us.

'He is not looking for me. For one or other twisted reason he is looking for YOU.' He flipped my cell phone on my lap.

Hundreds of miscalls and messages, all from Nick.

SAVE HAVEN

Without reading one message, I got out of the car, threw the cell phone down on the asphalt, stomping on it. Screaming like a mad thing. Never mind that the thing didn't break with the impact, just covers and stuff flying in all directions.

While I was acting like a lunatic, Cameron was silently plotting our next move. I was standing next to the road, contemplating the vast emptiness of the semi-dessert, when he draped his arm around me, kissing the top of my head.

'Feeling better, Short Stuff?' Playfully near crushed my ribs.

Poking him with my elbow, I snorted very unladylike. I had to admit that I actually did feel better.

'Cradock. I don not think he will look for us there, again. He will think we are stupid to return there. I am banking on his perception that we are clueless to his world.' He sounded bitter, but I also know him well enough not press for any explanations.

'Sure, Big Brother! You lead and I will follow,' trying to inject a little humor into the situation.

He gave me another squeeze and pushed me towards the car.

There he unceremoniously took out the little that I had and threw it into the culvert.

'HEYYY!'

I was too late to stop him. When he did the same with his stuff, I quit complaining.

He upended my sling bag, throwing creams and lotions over his shoulder. The paper stuff like my identity document, drivers' license and notebook, he tore in little pieces, setting it on fire on the road.

While I was staring at the little fire, Cameron was making a few calls on his cell. I was not surprised by the fact that he changed from English to Afrikaans fluently.

We watched silently until the slight breeze blew the last bit of ashes away.

Taking out the simcard of his cell, picking out mine in the debris of mine, he took out the multi-purpose knife he carried and snipped it into little pieces. Then he also demolished is cell under his heel.

'There, the first step to a new life.'

NEW IDENTITY

Not really understanding what he meant by that but trusting him to do what is best for us.

The drive was silent, until we nearly reached the town, our new home. Cameron took a turn to the left, driving down a dust road, nearly rattling my teeth from my head.

When he slowed and parked near a ramshackle house I was a bit surprised.

A man came out the door, his appearance not fitting to his surroundings.

Cameron squeezed my hand.

'If Rupert has done his job, we would soon be other people.'

Getting out of the car he walked towards the man, shaking hands briefly. I could not hear what passed between them, but I did see a bundle of notes changed from Cameron's to the man who handed him, judging from the color, passports and identity books, with several cards.

Not long after that Cameron came back to the car, the man disappearing behind the house and soon speeding past us in a powerful motorbike.

Sorting between the documents, Cameron handed me a passport, identity book and a debit and credit card.

'Hey! But this is…'

'Yes, it is. But you are not taking over her identity or her name. You will carry the same names, but with different identity numbers. That way we can avert too much confusion. She don't mind a bit. In fact, she is laughing her head of.' Giving one of his rare smiles. 'And the fact that you two look nearly identical, clinched the deal. The names is pronounced the same, but spelled differently in your documents.'

He looked at his watch.

'In exactly 8 hours, Caren Christine McBride and Cameron Nicholson will cease to exist. We would be wiped out from the South African database. No documents was ever issued to those two names, no bank accounts were opened, no business was ever done by them, nothing! As if we were never born, never existed.'

He lifted his eyebrow laconically.

'It is not as if the names we had were ever our own.'

STARTING OVER

It was with a whole lot of trepidation that I followed Cameron into the house. Memories assailed me, good and bad. Surprisingly, the good ones were more.

Ma loved this little house, so cozy and compact. The thick walls muted the sounds from outside, keeping the house cool. The interior was different, not one piece of furniture the same as it was before.

'I had an alarm installed. There is motion sensors in all the rooms, so be sure to turn it of when u enter, and turn it back on when you leave. All the windows have pressure pads. The same rule applies; turn it of before you open. I hired two guards for 24-hour surveillance. By the first scream of the alarm, one or both will be here within two minutes. If the electricity goes of, the system is powered by a battery-pack, kept loaded by a sun panel. The wiring is replaced, so if you ever notice any wires out in the open, press the panic button.'

He handed me a bunch of keys.

'Be sure to turn the key FOUR times and then once back when you lock the front door, the same with the kitchen door. The doors will be replaced soon.'

'Caren, I cannot stress enough that your life would be totally different than it was before. You will NOT be able to design again. You will NOT be able to contact any of your friends or business partners ever again. That part of your life is over. We have a few months until we can use the cards and our new bank accounts. Until then I have enough cash to see us through. I would suggest that we leave this house at the minimum. We have food stocked. Bread and milk will be delivered, and anything else you may need.'

That was the longest speech I ever heard him give. That fact, more than anything else, impressed the seriousness of my situation.

You are going to leave me here alone?' I struggled to keep the panic from my voice.

'I have to act normal, Sis. Go back to the farm. Do what I always do. He will be sure to look for you with me. We cannot take that chance. But I will be here when the workmen come to replace the doors. And Danica and her grandmother will be here in a few months. The old lady has cancer, and she prefers to get her radiation here. Make me a cup of sludge before I leave.'

I was terrified at being left alone. I also know that he was right. Whatever Nick's planes were, it did not include Cameron.

Even though I was used to being alone, earning a living, this situation is fearsome.

SETTLING IN

It was a difficult time for me.

Being used to be around people, the silence of the house was getting to me. The fact that I couldn't cook was another.

If it wasn't for Danica's old computer, I would have been loco within the week.

Between guzzling my sludge (that was what Cameron and Ma dubbed my coffee) and pre-cooked meals, I got acquainted with the Internet.

I never had the fascination with the 'global community' like Ma did. I soon saw why she found it so... mesmerizing.

True to the promise I made to Cameron about being careful, I connected to the Internet with the cell phone I found in the desk drawer, thankful that there was still available funds.

After a few false starts if figured it out and soon I discovered Google. What fun! Much better than the television I tried on my first day. I didn't even try the radio. Well, there was a lot of CD's, but music never held my attention, except what should be played on a fashion runway, or not.

At first I looked up the fashion pages, having mock arguments with the designers. My fingers itched to remake some of the designs, taking something of here, adding something else there. That was when my inability to draw frustrated me the most.

I used the dictionary. Let it fall open, closed my eyes and let my finger chose a word. The dictionary soon became spotted with grease spots, from my finger I dipped in my butter.

That's another thing about me that drove Ma to distraction. I loved butter. And every chance I got, I would take a tub from the freezer, and just dip my finger in it, lick it clean, sucking of the last bit of richness.

Ma always made sure that she had enough tubs of real butter after that. Margarine just didn't taste the same.

I am rambling again...

Well, that computer became my friend, my only link to the outside world. I never left the house. What I needed was delivered. When I wanted something more, I gave the order to the deliveryman. Always the same person.

DANICA

Danica and her grandmother arrived after a few weeks, right before the schools started. Even with my untrained eye I could see that her grandmother is very ill.

The next few days was a whirlwind of getting Danica ready for school, and her grandmother for her stint in the city hospital. The day before school started the ambulance took her grandmother to hospital. It was a tearful moment and Danica moped around the house for hours.

By the good graces Danica could cook! No more heating tasteless prefab dinners or opening cans!

We soon settled into a routine.

I, being the lazy one, sleeping in, with Danica cooking breakfast, leaving mine in the oven until such time I deemed necessary to eat. I will heat up a few packets for lunch and for dinner we will get something from the local restaurant.

For her it was absolute bliss. Where in the past ordering in was a treat, it became an institution.

She didn't have a lot of free time, trying to keep to the routine her mother set out for her when she was alive. School and study came first, then her martial arts and then hockey. She still is sport crazy!

Cameron called regularly on Danica's cell phone and he promised a visit before my birthday.

As usual, I forgot all about it. It just didn't FEEL like my birthday. But when my real birthday was I will never know.

Things changed after one day Danica came back from school very worried.

She was certain that she was being followed for quite a while by then, but that day she saw the man for the first time.

She didn't say anything to me, knowing that it would agitate me. But she did tell me that she is going to confront the man the next day. To ask him why he has been following her.

I tried to dissuade her. By God, she was only fourteen! How would she defend herself against a grown man?

I needn't have worried.

TURNING POINT

There was not much sleep for us that night.

In spite of all the alarms, Danica and I just couldn't sleep long enough to get enough rest.

As usual she was up and on the go at five in the morning. This time taking extra care to how she is wearing her school uniform. Nothing that can flap and hinder any sudden movement, her hair made up in a braid, out of her face.

Breakfast was all our favorite things but we didn't do it any justice. Her cat was in 7th heaven with all the leftovers.

When she left for school, I watched her through the spy hole until she turned I couldn't see her anymore. She looked casual, no worries in the world, her usual self.

I was left alone, jumping at every sound, biting my nails to the quick. It was nerve racking. Even the clock had a grudge against me, going as slow as molasses on a cold winters night.

Distracting myself with the computer didn't work. Not even doing the dishes or cleaning the house. I must have been supercharged. I remember not even an hour had passed between the time I had started and when I finished.

The house was sparkly clean and I still had a few hours to go.

It turned out I didn't have to wait that long.

Hours before the school should be out, the key turned in the door. I was near screaming my head of, remembering soon that any other combination in turning the key would set of the alarm.

I was very glad to see Danica's disheveled face. A bit red from exertion, but filled with a glee that was totally strange to her. A dust mark on her face and her blouse untucked told its own story.

She won the day.

Her art stood her in good stead. The fact that it was so easy for her to break the man's arm, causing him enough pain to spill the beans, boosted her self-confidence.

My nightmare is back.

It was one of Nick's men.

FEARFUL DAYS

What passed between them, I still to this day not fully understand. She still refuses to talk to me about that day. That Nick sent him, was the only thing she told me.

Maybe it was because we looked like twins, me albeit a bit shorter, that made him follow her. Why else would Nick send someone to follow her, after all?

At first she stayed home, on the pretext that she was 'guarding' me. She didn't lie too well. I lacked the nerve to dig deeper.

Cameron promised to be with me on my birthday, but that day went past without much notice. I worried about him, but he was capable of looking after himself.

After a few days Danica decided that it is time to go back to school, confident that she will be able to defend herself if something untoward happens.

Being alone again during the days left me with too much time thinking.

To this day I know there will never be a clear answer to all my questions. Certainly not to the one that kept turning over and over in my mind.

'WHY?'

Why would Nick do all those terrible things?

I am still a child, I didn't do anything to him. What could I have done that made him so angry?

The biggest question of all: Why did MA die? How?

I was sure that Cameron had all the answers.

Danica tried to call him several times, but his voice-mail was on. I tried to worry too much, knowing Cameron would have a valid reason.

But that knowledge didn't still the unease that gnawed inside me.

When Danica returned from school smiling, I tried to pick up our routine. I shoved the unpleasant incident behind me.

Cameron still didn't call.

A week after my birthday my newfound peace and quiet was shattered. In a few insane minutes, my life changed forever.

MADNESS

Danica prepared breakfast as usual. That morning I decided to eat with her. Feeling quite upbeat because Cameron at last called in, I quickly cleaned the house of any dust-bunnies, neatening up an already neat house.

The computer didn't interest me, so I decided to take a nap. I weren't tired, but I know with Cameron there, we would go to bed very late that night.

I was dozing when the doorbell rang. Not expecting any deliveries that morning, I decided to ignore it. Then the person on the other side of the door started knocking and then pounding on the door.

I was quite pissed. Didn't that person know that nobody is home when a doorbell went unanswered? I got up, determined to give that person a piece of my mind.

I just reached my bedroom door that leads directly to the kitchen that the front door shattered.

Shocked, I saw Nick in the short corridor.

This is most difficult for me to write. The moment is still as clear as glass in my mind, but at the same time I cannot make sense of what I saw and what happened. I will try to be as clear and concise as I can be. Most of the details I heard from Cameron, Danica and the police that was a thorn in my side for a long time afterwards.

It was quite clear that Nick was very agitated and angry. He did not look like the suave sophisticated businessman he was. His hair was standing on end, his suit dirty and wrinkled. He had a wild look in his eyes and his whole frame was shaking.

The thing that shocked me most was the gun in his hand.

'Wanda! Oh my god! I found you! Please baby come back to me! I promise I will be good! I promise!' His voice was hoarse and shaky and I remember I was fascinated by the little drop of spit that rolled down his chin.

'Uncle Nick, it's me, Caren. Ma died a few months ago, don't you remember?'

I swear I tried to speak clearly. I swear!

'Don't lie, you bitch! You come back to me now! Or I swear I will kill you right where you are! You belong to me! No other man will ever have you! EVER!'

The last word was a high-pitched scream, so unlike the soft-spoken man I knew.

I was shocked, frozen where I stand. I remember opening my mouth to speak, reason with him. I remember I lifted my hands, but it was like something kept me rooted, not able to speak or move.

When he didn't get the reaction he wanted, Nick pointed the gun at me. Maybe I should be glad that his hand was shaking. Maybe I should be happy that his aim was of. Maybe I should be happy that he used soft nosed bullets in his gun.

I am not.

The first shot went wild, hitting the ceiling.

The second shot ricochet at an angle against the wall behind me, changed direction, and hit me in my lower back, slamming me down.

The third shot went of while I was on my way down, hitting me just beneath my breast.

I don't remember feeling any pain. Just my ears screaming from the noise of the shots fired, booming in the small kitchen.

I remember lifting my head, looking up at Nick.

I remember seeing James behind Nick, who was pointing his gun straight in my face, ready to pull the trigger again.

I remember the gun in James's hand. I remember seeing Nick stumble, blood on his leg. I remember seeing Nick still staring at me, ready to fire again, not even in his madness registering that he himself was shot.

I remember James' agonized face when he stepped forward, hitting Nick on the head with the butt of the gun. I remember Nick not even blinking an eye.

I remember Nick lowering the gun an inch, his finger whitening on the trigger.

I remember James aiming his gun at Nick's head, his mouth screaming.

I remember the moment when James fired his gun, killing Nick.

I remember Nick falling, stumbling by the impact.

I remember the look in his eyes. Stunned, then lifeless, a few inches from my face.

I remember watching the blood pooling between us.

Then, mercifully, just the merciful blankness and darkness of nothing at all.

LOST DAYS

I really don't remember much of my stay in hospital. Quite frankly, I do not WANT to remember anything of that time.

I woke up in a panic, not being able to move at all. I struggled, but it was like a lead weight was pressing me down.

My first impression when I finally opened my eyes was that I was upside down. The only thing I could see was the greenish bluish carpet on the floor. I tried to turn my head and a fresh wave of pain shot through my body.

The next moment Cameron peered at me, his serious face calmed me.

'You decided to wake up then,' giving me one of his rare smiles while he pressed a red button near my head. 'just stay calm, the nurse will be here soon.'

It was not long before a whole troop of them marched into the room, turning me right side up and started to fiddle and prod me. Bags were removed and replaced with new ones.

It was when one nurse remarked that they will not remove the tube from my throat just yet, that I noticed for the first time that I was not breathing on my own. That the soft swish-click was that of a ventilator.

I was in a cage or something. LOOKED like a cage. Not really though. It was more like a bed in hoops. I was tied to it by the head and my arms. I tried to move my legs but couldn't. I thought it was tied down too.

Until Cameron sat by me, took my hand, and told me what happened.

They had to remove a part of my left lung, the exploding bullet doing the most damage there. They removed as much lead as they could. They also had to work fast as I had an adverse reaction to the anesthetic.

My lower back was damaged. They had to remove part of my intestines as well as my uterus and one fallopian tube. I was pretty well cut up.

I was out for nearly three weeks.

When Cameron's words finally sank in, I realized that I am never going to walk again. Never be able to have my own babies. Never have a normal life again.

That was too much. I was not prepared to accept that. I blacked out again.

SELF PRESERVATION

I tried to ignore my.. uhhh… illness to the best of my ability. That's not saying much, I know.

Try to think of it this way: Would u rather remember the bad? Or the good things?

I went a bit too far I think, I forgot most of it. The good included. I turned surly, impatient and totally unreasonable.

While my voice was still hoarse and scratchy, I gave into screaming fits when I didn't get my way. Well, once the tube was removed from my throat, that is.

I refused therapy. I demanded more freedom for my arms and hands. I insisted they took of the metal thing around my head. Cameron had to sign various releases as the doctors and nurses refused to take responsibility for any aggravating injuries.

I didn't give a horse's feather.

Cameron indulged me, but he also warned me what the results may be if I didn't take the doctor's advice. My response was that nothing anybody could do, will let me walk again.

My life had ended.

Making an end of the useless existence wouldn't have worked, not in a hospital. I was watched too closely. I was determined to make an end of it. That time will come soon enough.

I didn't see Cameron much after the first few weeks.

Once in a while he would come and just stay for an hour, sometimes even less.

On one of these visits he told me that James were not charged with Nick's murder, as he had to do it to save my life.

James, the softhearted giant, once against me, saved my life. At that moment I hated him. What kind of life did he save me from? Irrationally I wished him dead.

A few weeks later he committed suicide. Maybe because he couldn't resolve the fact that he took another man's life.

I still have that nagging thought that I was partly responsible, for having refused to see him. His death is on my conscience till this day.

LOSE ENDS

When Cameron first told me that Nick's parents wanted to visit, I refused outright. I didn't want any reminders of that man who put me there.

The only one I wanted to see was Cameron. It felt he was the only person I could trust. I knew he was busy. Packing up Ma's stuff and carting it home.

What I didn't know was that Cameron was driven by his own devils.

He told me on his previous visit that Tom Middleton requested his presence with the reading of Nick's will.

A week would normally have been between his visits, but this time he stayed away longer. At first I worried, until I reminded myself that he was a grown man, and used to looking after himself.

In the meantime I concentrated on getting well enough to leave hospital. I had not given up on the idea of terminating my useless existence. My thinking was quite clear and rational at that time.

That's what I thought at least. I had no idea that I had fallen into a deep depression.

When Cameron at last came to visit, he looked morose and unhappy. The lines were clearly etched on his face. He was unnaturally quiet, more than he normally was.

If I thought that my strange and twisted life was settled, I was very fast divested of the notion.

Whatever he had to say will not come easy. Cameron never had the problem of speaking his mind. So whatever he had to tell me then, weighed him down. But even I didn't expect the words that left his mouth.

'I am not Cameron Nicholson. My real name is Cameron Mitchel Willcott. Nicholas Willcott was my father.' With that words he got up, gave my hand a squeeze, and left.

I was shocked. I believe I didn't breathe for a few minutes. Not having the Willcott's visit, were not ridding me of my demons.

My brother, whom I loved so much, was part of the man that destroyed my life.

For the first time since I was shot, I burst into tears.

I was truly alone.

FACING FACTS

Well, that was that. I didn't expect to ever saw my brother again.

I couldn't have been more wrong.

While I was drenching myself in self-pity, Cameron was busy ensuring that I would be safe.

What he didn't tell me, was that Tom Middleton was after me. Just as mad and crazy as his boss with a bloodlust to match.

Nicholas Willcott was a pussycat compared to Tom Middleton. Tom Middleton loved killing. Maybe that was the only time he ever smiled, the moment when the last breath left his victims.

Not for one moment I thought about what and how Cameron must be feeling. In one moment his life changed forever. And I didn't waste one moment thinking of that.

Why should I?

HE was the one that fell with his hiney into pure butter! He already had the farm, and now he inherited Nick's enormous estate.

He would be stinking rich and I as poor as a church mouse, with no way of accessing my money, because Caren Christine McBride did not exist anymore. I was left destitute, having to rely on other people to pay my accounts, keeping me alive.

That thought just strengthened my resolve in ending it all. Whatever was there to live for anyways?

Not a devil's whisker.

One after the other, I am losing everything that ever meant anything in my life.

All due to the Willcotts.

My hatred for the whole family grew to breaking point.

One way or the other, SOMEONE was going to pay for what happened to me. Preferably taking the whole stinking lot with me.

That's the fact: I was stone-cold, nothing on earth could have turned me then from my purpose.

GOING HOME

I was in hospital for 4 months.

It was like the time didn't want to pass. It was terrible. Anxious to get home, to formulate my plans, do what I wanted.

Yes, my feelings towards Cameron DID change. How else? He was always there to help me, never lifting a finger in anger. He was surely the only person I could trust.

He couldn't help that his biological father was a criminal and a killer. I know that it was in him to become that, having that closed side of him.

The fact that Ma raised him must have made the difference, or good genes from his mother.

He was my brother, and I loved him.

The day he came to fetch me, was also the first time I noticed the two men outside my door. It was when they followed us outside, covering us, the one making sure the way ahead is 'clean', searching the car for heaven knows what, that I know there were more going on than Cameron told me.

He had that closed look on his face again.

The two men both got into different cars, the one moved in front of us, the other followed us.

I was tense the whole time until we reached home.

Even there the changes were very visible. No longer a sweet little house in the middle of a historic street in a quaint little town, but a veritable fortress.

Someone had to be very clever or foolish to have tried to get over the blade-wire enforcements on the 6-feet walls around the house. Even the gate in front was re-enforced. The front door opened with the old key, but on the inside was another door, steel, and very heavy. On the inside there were 4 locks, and a die bolt swift-lock.

The windows were covered with heavy mesh. There was no way anybody could enter there!

My room looked the same, but not.

Cameron pulled open my desk drawer, showing me a small gun. For when all else fails.

49

RETHINKING STUFF

Cameron took to coming and going. After that shocking disclosure in the hospital, we didn't discuss his parentage at all. Our conversations bordered on the polite. It was like we didn't know what to say to each other.

Danica tried to maintain her seriously cheerfulness. It was as if she decided that she would be the light breeze on an otherwise hot day.

It worked.

She had me smiling again. Sometimes I had to suppress the lightness that threatened to take away my resolve.

When her grandmother was well enough to leave the hospital after her treatments, they left again.

Without her as a buffer, things between Cameron and me became a little bit more strained. I felt secure that my brother loved me, and I knew that I loved him too. But there was that divide between us and neither of us knew how to cross it.

When the last of Ma's boxes were stashed in the living room, Cameron spoke out at last.

'I will not be coming around so much anymore. This afternoon three people will come here to be introduced to you. They will look after you. I expect you to listen to them and do as they say. And it's time you start with your therapy.'

He didn't give me a chance to protest or say anything, because right on cue, the outside gate's bell rang.

If Cameron thought about covering the indigenous people of South Africa, he did it right. But I knew my brother, he would have looked for the most loyal, the best at their trade, not been influenced by race, color or creed.

A small colored girl for cleaning and cooking, a enormously large and tall black woman as my nurse, and if I was so inclined, a handsome white young doctor, to monitor my health.

During the introductions Cameron had a firm grip on my shoulder, knowing that I would have bolted.

My fear of people reared its ugly head and my mind shut down.

When I came to I was in my bed, my new entourage arranged around it.

__CHANGES__

Cameron left, leaving me to face the strangers alone. I suppressed my panic. Cameron knew that I would have to accept these people or else die before I was ready to do so.

My refusal to take therapy had a few bad consequences. I was still fed intravenously and still carry a fitting for a colostomy bag if and when I decided to eat again.

I am sure they DO have real names, but I still have a problem with my short-term memory. I am sure somewhere in the future I will remember it.

I renamed the maid 'Ninnie' because she have an insane sense of humor. The smallest thing would set her of laughing, even my anger. Stupid Ninnie!

She would cook the most delicious food. No matter what I did, I was getting back my appetite. The one thing I did have, was my coffee and my butter.

I was not planning to eat, well, not soon anyways. But she sure did know how to tempt me!

I took to calling the nurse, Maria. She did have another name, as did Doc. Ninnie, Maria and Doc.

Over the next few months we would become good friends. However, I wasn't impressed. I saw it as another complication in my life.

Doc visited every morning. Do that 'check-up' thingy of him. Prick my finger for a blood sample, take my blood pressure, listened to my lungs, that kind of stuff.

It was irritating at most. And when Maria started to massage my legs and forced me into light exercises, I almost blew my top.

I also realized that working WITH, rather than against, would stood me in better stead to do what I want. So, I changed.

I did! On the outside I did, inside I still was this frightened little girl kicking around, screaming.

The first thing Doc did, was taking out the catheter, and hooking up the colostomy bag. First things first. A few days later he removed my feeding bag. That was what I called the IV.

I learned when it was time to go to the bathroom. With no feeling, it was terrible, a most difficult thing for me to learn. More than once I woke up in a wet bed, much to my disgust.

FINDING PEACE

I soon learned to recognize the signs and reactions of my 'new' body. I learned how to pee even when I didn't felt like it. I learned how to turn myself, how to move from my bed to the wheelchair without any help.

From massaging and light 'un-locking' exercises, Maria moved me to more strenuous therapy. Weight lifting, trying to walk between two parallel bars, resistance training, and all that stuff aimed at strengthening muscles not being able to work on their own anymore.

No sooner did I learn one thing, the next thing will pop up.

Like dressing myself. Now THAT was a total bore! I much preferred the loose hospital gowns.

But they had other ideas.

Jumpin' pockmarked jellyfish!

It was scarcely a few weeks later that Doc and a few friends were hammering and tinkering in my kitchen, much to the disgust of Ninnie, who had to clean up afterwards.

Doc and a few friends of his changed the whole kitchen. Made it accessible for someone in a wheelchair.

If he thought that THAT would cheer me up, he was sadly mistaken.

I was ordered to learn how to cook. I refused, of course! I was a disaster in the kitchen.

Slowly but surely I made progress. I was soon able to make coffee for myself and fetching my own butter.

I made a shaky pact with myself: get better as soon as possible, if only to get rid of the busybodies clucking around me.

I started surfing seriously in my free time. Playing online games, that kind of stuff. Not many of them really caught my attention and I soon got bored with it.

I tried chat rooms, but that was a total disaster. The people I met there was mostly so dishonest I could have felt it thousands of miles away. And the rest, well, the least say the better.

I was just getting into my new routine, when disaster struck.

TRAGEDY

I was turning into a carefree soul again.

The therapy strengthened my formally unused muscles to sleek work engines. I was getting used to doing exercises. I challenged myself to do more, upping the weights and time spent on the machines.

I would laugh and joke with my three jailers. Even once getting a spanking from Maria for throwing a tantrum when things didn't went the way I wanted, being rude and disrespectful.

I still giggle about that! I never expected it! Afterwards I accused her of being a bully, knowing full well that I have no way of defending myself. She just smirked and assured me that being disrespectful and rude will earn me a spanking any day, so I had to watch my mouth.

The last time I saw Cameron he stressed the fact that I should be careful. He was always serious, but this time I noticed a note of urgency in his voice. I assured him that I always check everything.

Actually, it was Ninnie that took over the job of checking all the windows and doors, making sure nothing was tampered with, listening for the locks to click five times, before closing the last one behind her.

I was safe.

A week later my cell rang in the wee hours of the morning. It was Cameron, and for the first time since I knew him, there was panic in his voice.

'Caren! I don't have any time to explain. I am at the gas station filling up. I am being followed and don't want to take the chance of Tom Middleton finding you! BE CAREFUL! I will contact you as soon as I can. I love you Sis!'

That was his last words to me. I was so sure that Cameron could look after himself, that I went back to sleep.

The next morning when I opened the door for Doc, I could see that something was wrong.

I was right.

Cameron was dead.

Crashed his bike at high speed in a truck that lost traction on the wet road.

MISERY

The next few days were pure misery.

Doc had to smuggle me into the morgue to identify Cameron.

I will never forget that sight. It became part of my nightmares.

Even tough Doc prepared me of how Cameron would look; nothing can really prepare anyone seeing the dead body of a loved one.

I could see that his body was in pieces, the blood-covered sheet unable to hide the fact. Doc tried to hide most of the damage done to Cameron, hiding most of his head in a towel.

His eyes were taped shut and somebody tried to clean his face. But the damage was clearly visible. It looked like his head popped, the bones re-arranged in a haphazard way. His skin was abraded on the one side, the other side clear and untouched, just swollen out of proportion.

There was no doubt that it was my brother.

I was thankful for the tranquilizer Doc gave me before we left the house. Strangely, I did not go mad. Instead I became ice-cold, it felt like my skin was too tight for my body. I do not know how to describe it. It was like a million bugs were crawling just under my skin.

'He should be with Ma, on the farm.'

Doc tried to give me a hug but I shrugged him off.

'It looks like you know more about the circumstances around my family than I do. Be sure you have all the facts. I want to know everything.'

If I thought I was alone, that day it became true. I was back to where I once was. Poor little girl, everyone dead around her. No one left.

The difference were that I am eight years older and crippled.

I thought I would have been much better of if Wanda Parker did not picked me of the street.

I would have survived, I think. Maybe totally degraded as a person, but at least I still would have had my legs.

GETTING THE FACTS

I was right, Doc indeed knew Cameron. And the old Willcotts. I would have met him along time ago if I stayed home with Ma.

And he knew the circumstances around Ma's death.

Yeah, I know.

I have been living my life the way I deemed fit. I saw then that I was merely hiding my head in the ground, like an ostrich.

I was still running from reality. Problems? No such thing! I ignored anything that would have rattled my golden cage. I didn't cultivate any friendships, that would have taken too much... giving! Of opening up, explore my personality. Share it with someone.

Was it my early years that made me like that? I don't know. My shrink doesn't know, but think it highly probable.

I digress..

Doc first met Cameron a few weeks after he left us the first time, when he found his biological grandparents. I guess I will never know what happened to his mother. Cameron had a cut in one of his feet that didn't heal well, even with conventional medicine.

Doc was doing his two-year stint for the government, before embarking on his research into tropical diseases, that being his first love. Over time he kept up with his studies, but found a deep-seated satisfaction in his practice as a small town clinic doctor.

It seems that Cameron took an immediate liking to the young doctor, and went as far to introduce him to Ma, who took to him just as fast.

Now, Ma always had an eye for a nice-lookin' man, and Doc fitted the bill to a tee. I am sure Ma never overstepped her bounds, her being so much older than Doc, and still in love with that man.

Ma never did get better after she left hospital. According to Doc, Cameron told him that she refused to eat and that she fed intravenously. She didn't have the will to life any more.

Even after her 'forced' marriage to Nick to protect that man, she refused food. Even regurgitating the little bit they forced into her throat with a tube.

A few weeks later she was found dead in her bed. She bled to death after pulling out the needles and tubes that kept her alive and, accidentally or on purpose, tearing her fragile skin and veins.

Of the obsessive love Nick had for Ma, I already knew about that, even if a few bullets drummed it into me.

I had no doubt that Nick got 'rid' of Ma's boyfriends, whether by buying them of, or by any other means.

Her death made him go nuts. The possibility of never having Ma around were just not acceptable to him. He was really out of his mind with grief.

Cameron had to spirit Ma's body away while Nick was in one of his drunken stupors, with the ever present Tom Middleton by his side.

In his mind Nick could not accept Ma's death. When he went to her room, not finding her there, he went on a rampage, looking for her.

And found me.

Everyone that ever saw me, Ma and Danica together, would have believed we were family. We all had the same bone structure, the white skin that can't take any sun, although Danica was by far the tallest of us, me topping ma with an inch or two.

Even when the damage his fist made to my face, I must have looked like Ma. My inability to placate him cost me my health, and his life.

And that of poor James.

Tom Middleton swore to wipe out what was left of our family. Cameron and me.

Though he did calmed down after the will of Nick Willcott revealed that Cameron was his son. Why Cameron's mother saw fit to throw her baby in a rubbish heap, rather than let Nick know that he had a son, I would never know.

But I can make a pretty good guess.

According to Doc, Cameron refused to accept his inheritance. Nick's lawyer and partner assured Cameron that he do have a few weeks to think it over, before anything was finalized.

As far as I know, and Doc, Cameron never touched that money.

I expected it to go to the next of kin, the older Willcotts.

56

Doc also revealed that Cameron was running from Tom Middleton the night he died. Cameron took to the habit of ever changing the cars or bikes he used to visit me.

That night Cameron were with Doc, filling him in, asking him to look after me. He also told Doc that the older Willcotts would pay my bills, medical or otherwise. That a monthly amount would be paid into his account to take care of it.

Why Cameron used a bike in pouring rain, only he would know.

He called me from the gas station, cautioning me again and again. And he told me he loved me.

He sped away from town, Tom Middleton in hot pursuit, seeing too late the swerving truck across the road. Smashed into it at high speed. Tore him to pieces.

Doc also informed me that Maria worked in his surgery, and that Ninnie was from the farm. Cameron knew them all personally and trusted them implicitly.

That I figured out myself, not being an idiot an' all. Cameron would never allow anyone he don't trust near me. Not while I was acting like an immature little girl, not knowing what to do next.

I learned fast.

Cameron's death was the turning point in my life.

For the first time in years I had to accept the fact I was well and truly alone, no one to fall back on, no one to moan and rant and rave with about the unfairness of life.

I do have his friends, but they were not family.

I refused Doc's offer of more tranquilizers, preferring to be clearheaded, thinking about my future.

I have this house, but no money. My bills are taken care of. Everything I want or need, would be paid by others.

There would be a lot for me to do, my therapy and stuff.

And the boxes full of Ma's stuff.

I had a fleeting thought that maybe there would be something in it of my real family.

See?

My brother was not long dead, and already I was looking for my next crutch.

FACING UP

After that talk with Doc, I fell into my mute and stubborn stage.

When Ma found me, I was a quiet, serious girl. Maybe from the stuff and things I saw on the street. First watching my father die, then my mother. Now, years later, I would not wish that years on my worst enemy.

Maybe the peace, love and quiet I found at Ma's tempered me a little bit, making me want what she had. All I knew was that I would never go back there.

But living on charity was not an option.

I was thinking about making clothes again, but Doc cautioned me to keep a low profile until we were sure that Tom Middleton has given up on his search for me.

I did not realized that I was falling into depression, though I am sure that Doc saw.

I threw myself into therapy, tried to get as strong as I possibly could. I would swallow the medicine that Doc would hold out to me, not giving it a second thought.

Until I realized that I slept away days, only waking to eat and exercise. When I challenged him on it, he admitted to it, saying I needed the rest.

I turned to my computer again, but the games did not interest me anymore. Instead I googled on suicide. And the best way to go about it.

Poison seemed to be the weapon of choice but I didn't have access to any poisons. A quick survey of my new cupboards confirm it.

And I found a bottle of whiskey. I do not drink, well; I do, but very rarely. Like the time I was angry at Ma, got drunk on the collection of liquor in Nick's house, and then crashed my car leaving the estate.

What a bummer!

Being drunk only hurt myself, not anyone else. Though the only damage was to my little car, a heap of scrap metal wrapped around the old tree at the gate.

What I also found was a sharp little knife. Didn't know then what it was being used for and don't know now.

The blade was seriously sharp.

I have found the way.

PREPARATIONS

I had everything ready. The little knife was stashed in my drawer, way back; with the gun Cameron gave me for protection.

That made me thought of using the gun instead, but I gave up on that idea. I didn't like the idea of messing myself up, waking from another shot. In any case, I wasn't very sure where exactly to point the gun to get the best effect.

Anyways, the thought of blood and brains spattered all over the room wasn't very nice. So I got on the computer again, searching for a way of offing myself by cutting.

Anyone of you ever done that?

I was grossly interested in the stories about suicide. About the attempts and the stories behind it. The guilt of family members that were left behind. I had no family. All were dead. So no worries there.

The best way it seems to cut would be in the wrists. Then not a horizontal slash, but a vertical one, deep, slicing open the arteries.

I was amazed at the wealth of information available, free and ready for any tortured soul. I could see how easy it would be to follow that advice.

I also read that most successful suicides were on the spur of the moment. A great percentage of people, thinking about suicide, even planning it, never do it. That mostly it was only a cry for help.

I did not need any help. I wanted to die. There would be nobody to mourn my death. Maybe Tom Middleton would throw a party in my honor, his promise fulfilled.

I was just waiting for the right time.

That came soon enough.

But I hesitated.

I did not want to die alone.

Not that I want any one with me, just that I wanted to talk with someone while doing it. Like in a chat room.

I opened my dictionary and pointed.

'PIMP'

MISCONCEPTIONS

Never in my whole life did I suspect that such games exist!

It was an eye opening experience just surfing through the different sites. I was more attracted to the factual at first, but got bored fast. It was WORK for the poor women, the men getting the better deal. Not a very good way of earning a living.

The games were basically the same. Some were so elaborate that it would take years to figure it out. I did find the perfect game. Playing it on and off until I had a better understanding, getting fed-up when I was attacked, until I figured out how to protect myself.

I got a bit sidetracked from my original plans, enjoying the game. Getting tips from older players, finding the game a bit more involved than I previously thought.

I knew that if I clicked on that link for the chat room, I would see my plan through.

I took out the knife daily, running my finger over the sharp blade, earning me quite a few nicks along the way.

Everything was ready. I just have to do it.

The Americans surprised me. I expected less of them. I expected a stuck-up lot, vain and full of poo being a part of one of the mightiest nations.

Instead I found a likeable people, straightforward and honest. That there were a lot of exaggeration, that's to be expected, but all done in good clean fun. Exploits were blown up out of proportion and cussing were the order of the day.

I laughed.

For the first time in nearly a year, those people made me laugh. They made me believe that I was SOMEONE, not just a reject of society; which one of them did accuse me of.

That did hurt, brought out my past as a street child, a beggar on the streets.

I loved being there. The lighthearted banter lifted me out of my depression, making me want to live again.

Depression is a sneaky devil, creeping up in a person when least expected. After weeks of fun, it hit me again.

That time there were nothing to lift me out of my trip in self-pity. I was still my sparkly self in chat; only one person noticed that something was wrong.

MAKING THE EFFORT

He wrote me a private message, told me not to do what I am planning.

How did he know?

By that time I had already made the first cut, bleeding profusely. I tried to divert his attention, not admitting and even denying that I was considering suicide.

In the end I relented, wrapping the towel around my arm, calling Doc.

Doc were furious. With himself and me, for not noticing the signs of depression. He written it of as a normal reaction if grief.

He tried to get me to hospital but I refused. To do what there? He relented, not wanting to use force removing me and with the possible threat of Tom Middleton still hanging over my head.

I was thankful of the reprieve, though I was still weak from blood loss. That was easily remedied with enough sleep and rest, my natural instincts to survive doing the work.

My arm was painful and stiff, however, that did not stop Maria from doing her worst. She grew relentless, pushing me beyond my borders, then pushed again.

In a strange way I relished the challenges she threw at me. I never once tried to figure out WHY I were pushed so hard. Its not that I will ever walk again!

After the debacle of the unsuccessful suicide, Doc insisted I see a shrink. I resisted the idea, mostly because of meeting another stranger.

Without any pressure Doc brought his friend along under the guise of trying out my 'sludge'. That was a perfect opening.

The poor man tried his best, but couldn't swallow more than a few sips at best. It threw me into a fit of giggles and Doc soon followed me with a full-hearted roar of laughter.

We spent the time talking about my unsuccessful attempts at cooking, my love for eating butter out of the tub, and my most wonderful creation called 'sludge'.

My coffee sure had the power to break ice!

In subsequent visits, he came to like it, with lots of sugar and cream, not black and straight-up like I do.

Frog and me became firm friends.

FROG

I have this problem with names. Just can't remember it. So I make up names for the people I meet. Not just any name, it had to fit the individual.

Ninnie because she is always laughing. Life is a pleasure for her and she is living it full out. No half measures. No matter how bad a person or a situation, she will find the bit of good in it.

Maria, the motherly type. No nonsense. She will form her opinion on first glance, amending as she go along. She walks the straight path. Everything has a purpose, and that purpose must be fulfilled. Strictly religious.

She was the one who threw my priest out of the house, by his EAR, after being excommunicated by him and my church, for not being willing to confess my sins.

She was totally disgusted.

'YOUR sins?' she would gesture and exclaim about the totally unfairness of the Catholic Church. 'Ma bebbie got the lead and she made the sin?'

She have this way of talking, not familiar in the English language, but trying her best. She speaks Afrikaans fluently, and took it on herself to educate me in that 'civilized' language.

She didn't think nothing of getting rid of her clothes to get me out of the shower when I slipped and fell once, hitting my head quite badly.

The picture of her, enormously built, her length, this giant of a woman, 'AUW-AUWing', throwing of her clothes, filling my poor shower, to check me out for more serious injuries before lifting me up and swaddling me in a big towel.

That selfsame towel that looked like a washcloth against her giant body.

Oh my goodness! The image still sends me into fits of laughter, hurting my poor tummy!

And Doc is Doc. Too good-looking for my taste, muscular because he works out to keep fit. Being deemed too attractive to be a good doctor would drive him crazy! He hated that everyone judged him on his looks and not his abilities. He is an amazing healer.

Then came Frog.

I am NOT derogatory! He loves his nickname! Though I don't see him that often anymore. He did NOT look like a frog; it was his voice.

When in the evening, the frogs start with their song; there is always a frog with a deep croak. I am not sure that city folk would know what I am talking about, but that is the most beautiful sound in the country. That and the sound of crickets and sun bugs when the sun is burning outside.

Frog's voice sounded like that of the big frog.

He tried to get me to talk about my experiences, but one way or the other I just couldn't. He came up with the novel idea of giving me words, and let me make a sentence out of it. Or a description, whatever the case might have been.

My voice was bad. Rasping and wheezing I would force out sounds. I just gave up on talking. It was much easier communicating by writing down what I wanted to say.

He would ask a question, and I will type out the answer. It became fun.

It was then that he told me to write my story.

I did try, but it was like there were large gaps in my memory. Certain parts of my life would sent me in a panic, though I never could remember WHY.

Frog told me to start at the beginning; as far back as I can remember.

'But I never wrote a story before!'

'That's it! Start with that, and just let your mind do the talking. Don't even try to THINK, let your fingers remember!'

He was quite excited after reading that first page. He told me I had a real knack in describing things, but he wanted me to elaborate more.

I couldn't.

The words on the pages were from my fingers, remembering the bits and pieces of my life I couldn't bear to think of.

I have never read what I wrote. I leave that to others. I posted some of the chapters in a blog, and on a site of a friend.

It seems that they liked the story.

The story of my life became reading material. I prefer to let people thinking of it as fiction. I HATE sympathy!

DOING THE IMPOSSIBLE

I already told about how I met the love of my life.

Steven.

There is no words in any language to describe how I feel about him.

Even at impossible odds he were the only one to believe that I would ever walk again.

And walk I did.

Even if it was with a brace and a stroller.

Doc and Maria were elated, so was I.

Doc also confirmed though I had a lot of damage to the vertebrae, my spinal cord was not severed, and the changes were good of me walking again. Though the nerves did suffer a lot of damage.

When I gave my first uncertain step without the help of the bars, I actually cried.

The only person I could share my joy and accomplishment with was Steven. Though he still is the most important person in my life, I missed the friends I had made in the chat room.

For some reason or other they started to ignore me. That hurt a lot, but I never was one who begged for friendship. If they preferred to ignore me, it's their choice. But I wish I knew what I did wrong.

It was only recently that the man I owe my life to, accused me of lying and cheating. Only because my friend did what I asked her to do.

Although it hurt bad at the time, I realized that no one can decide another's thoughts and actions. What do I have to prove to them anyway? I supported his game, talked to no one except my teammates.

Well, I hope he did what I asked, and transferred the subs that were bought to the other players. If not, then I know he is the jerk other people accused him of being, caring for money only.

I pity him.

Still, there is a part of me thinking of him in a good way. If I could tell him in what name I live by, he can get his detective friends to search for me. Know that my life is not a farce.

There are a few others that I remember fondly, and I am glad that I knew them. Maybe we will have contact again in the future. I certainly hope so!

WOW!

I do go of at a tangent!

I was talking about me being able to walk again, and somehow or other good and bad times pop up.

Steven and I spent a lot of time together. Not a day will go by without at least telling the other what our day had been, and that our love is still standing strong, growing by leaps and bounds.

I discovered a side to me that was willing to change, to think of another person first. All due to Steven.

We talk about our hopes and dreams. We moan and groan about the unfairness of life.

We do fight.

That maybe one of the million reasons I love him so. He never think of me as disabled. When we disagree, and our conversation turn heated, he will give as good as he got, not afraid that I would crumble up in a little ball of self-pity.

I can write books about our short time together, the best time of my life. He supported me through everything, still do. And no matter how much I try, he refuses even to LOOK at another girl. In a leery way, off course!

That really makes me feel special, and loved. At times the wonder of it just wells up in me, making me feel that I can explode in pure happiness.

When the unforeseen happened, he was there.

I was getting too confident in my ability to walk, that I overdone it, slipped, and fell. If I had my stroller, I wouldn't have fallen.

But I did.

And damaged my back again.

Back to square one.

KEEPING TRACK

Well, that's recent events.

This is supposed to be therapy, writings and remembering of things past. Not a diary or a journal recording my life.

There is still a lot I want to tell.

Like the boxes with Ma's stuff

Like the letter from Cameron that I found and still not read.

Like Doc getting married.

And maybe more of Frog.

Frog is still my favorite. I miss his deep voice telling me to stop acting like a spoilt brat and get on with the thing called living.

And my cooking lessons.

Now THAT was disastrous!

Ninnie started out with my favorite foods, thinking that I will pick it up fast. After all, being of the weaker sex, women are born to cook and raise children!

Blegh!

Whoever came up with that stupid saying is hopefully frying in his own fat in hell.

I kept on making mistakes. Getting the food burned. Until Ninnie discovered that I moved away from the stove, doing things like playing games, basically anything, as long as its not hovering over a pot that refused to boil or fry or whatever.

I can still not make muffins.

There is still a dent in the plaster where I had thrown my last flop.

You guessed it; a rock is much weaker stuff than my muffins

That I forgot to mix in the eggs and baking powder doesn't matter a bit.

Muffins? I am not touching that recipe ever again. Point made.

MA'S BOXES

Now, I would be the first one to tell you what a wonderful caring person Ma was. Except for Oliver, not one of her boyfriends made any impact on me.

We didn't observe Christmas, except as a day of Church. No parties, no gifts. That never bothered me.

Nick would come over with lavish expensive gifts, which mostly ended up on the mantelpiece or in a cupboard, gathering dust.

Ma would prepare the most wonderful lunch. I always thought she was the best cook, until I discovered the plastic holders in the dustbin.

New Years Eve we would spent with the Willcotts, the grown-ups having a loud party and the children ensconced in a room with movies to watch, games to play and a bed to sleep on, if we couldn't keep our eyes open till midnight.

What Ma did on New Year, I found out when I unpacked the box marked 'cd's, etc' in Cameron's handwriting.

I never listened to music exclusively, just what I heard when I was at my stall. I never was interested enough to buy it.

Ma had a lot of music! And movies, on tape and on disc.

It was mostly music from the fifties up to the most contemporary. Even classical. I loved it.

That was the time that I seriously started to listen to music. The older, the better. Two types I really can't stand, and that is Rap and Jazz. UGHHHH!!!!

Music should tell a story, have a mood. Effect the listener. Yeah yeah. I became a sentimental fool. Loving 'mood' music.

But the thing that shocked me was the movies.

Ma, butt-naked, sloshing drinks. As drunk as a skunk. And all the people with her.

I was mortified!

WELL!

I bet there is not ONE child in this whole wide world, that can think of his or her parents having sex.

JUST RAMBLIN

I learned of another side of Ma.

That of a normal human being. I was always into myself, not really caring how others were living, experience life. As long as I was doing what I wanted, I was happy.

How do you define happiness?

Happiness for me then was enough money to do what I want, when I want. I was relentless in gathering my own money.

Ma kept my books in order. I am sure without her visiting me, picking up the loose cash I made for the day at my stall, and depositing it into a bank account, I would never have accumulated the nice little nest-egg.

I was quite careless with money. Ma kept a tight reign on it. When I thought I had lost everything, her friend at the local bank called on me, explaining what Ma had done. Investing a goodly sum every month, thus ensuring that I had something left for the future.

That was a nice surprise. And so like Ma.

Always thinking ahead.

In certain instances that is. She had atrocious taste in men. And lost everything, except the boxes Cameron packed. Like I mentioned earlier, Ma wasn't rich. The money she made was spend on the children she gathered, making sure that the kids had everything they wanted.

I did offer to pay Ma back for the money she spent in establishing me, and the apartment. She refused pointblank. Not even being sneaky in leaving a few notes laying around in her house could make her take it. She would always deposit the money into my account.

Ma was the best mother any child could wish for. Caring and protective and quite discerning in what a child want, or need.

Our wants was never ignored, but it was our needs that took first priority in her life.

Which was fine with us.

Being loved by Ma was as precious as any thing we ever wanted. For a street kid her love and attention was all we ever needed or wanted.

THE SEARCH

I got really excited when I found her journals. There was a lot of it.

Seems like Ma had kept a journal for nearly everyday of her life, from her student days. She really was very descriptive of her way of life and her feelings and emotions.

I felt very uncomfortable reading it. There was some pretty personal stuff in it.

After a lot of blushes and fidgettting and sometimes pure misbelieve, I decided to skip to the journals nearer the date Ma found me.

It seems like a good idea to search for an real family I may have. And all I had to go on was the tiny piece of paper in my pocket with my names on it.

Searching for McBrides on Google was time consuming and I soon felt like a dishrag. The only thing I was left with was enormous headaches from staring at the screen so long.

There were quite a few of them on the Internet, but none of them matched what I remembered of my real parents.

What I found in Ma's stuff was amazing.

Pictures.

Pictures of a younger Ma, but with long dark hair. Some of it just of her, others with a baby and later a young girl, about two, three years old.

The child could have been me the resemblance was so uncanny. Just three pictures with the child. It was then that I found Ma's reason for picking up street children to raise.

She has lost her own child.

For a few days I thought that I was Ma's real daughter. It was a heady time, until reality kicked in.

If I was that child, wouldn't Ma have said something? And the ever nosey Nick would sure have looked for me, if Ma had asked.

I decided to let it go.

Even if it would be nice to know where I came from, I can't rely on that information to change my life. I can pick up the pieces of my life and make something of it.

CONCLUSION

Well, this is my story.

My health is a bit dodgy and I am on constant surveillance. (Broad smile!) That's what I call it!

Frog is quite happy about my progress and only looks in once a month now. I always look forward to his visits. But if you ask me if I like him as a person, or just the sound of his voice, I will not be able to give you a straight answer.

NO! That is a very, very big lie!

I love that dear man. He is the only one that I allow to give me affectionate hugs. Maybe because he is so much older and he became the father I never had.

Not that I will tell him that! He would just come up with case studies of patients replacing him… blah blah BLAH!

I promise, next time I see him, I am going to tell him anyway. Tell him I love that ugly mug of his and will he adopt me?

He will throw a hissy fit!

I learned a lot from him. Especially on analyzing my actions. Think before I do and then do what I think is right. Recognize mistakes when I make them and do my best to right it. Always say I am sorry. Never hurt people intentionally.

And love life.

That last one is a bit tough.

Doc got married to a lovely girl. I have the feeling he is ready to move on, but his promise to Cameron keeps him here. And I am his favorite patient.

And Steven, who absolutely refuses to let me die.

There were a few instances where I was on the brink, like a few weeks ago, when I slipped into a coma when my kidneys packed up.

I just get tired sometimes, you know? Just feels like I want to go to sleep and not wake up.

I miss Ma and Cameron terribly, but Steven is my future. I am doing my best for him, because I love him.

THE END

Any incorrect spelling and wrong tenses is was were my own doing.... ☺

Not really… I am adding something Steven has written on my request!

Love you, sweet man!

EPILOGUE

I decided to join the chat room. I never had before, and didn't really have a reason to.

What business could I possibly have in some chat room for a game I didn't even play. I knew some of the people in there of course from elsewhere but most of them were new....people I'd never seen before, that weren't part of my game or its world.

For the first few days I was pretty quiet, more observing and speaking when needed than being the center of the party or anything.

There was one person I noticed more than the others though. That's when I started reading her story. I didn't know if it was real or fiction. I didn't care. It touched me and I felt different when I read it.

When I finished reading what there was of it (it wasn't complete) I decided to talk to the Author. She was the one I'd noticed in the room. Started out saying hi, a little of this and a little of that; trying to mix in with the rest of the room.

Very quickly I came to the conclusion that I wanted to be with this girl. We began talking more and more and eventually went to what I thought were private conversations. Later I found out she liked me and was nervous so she got a friend to help her talk to me.

I enjoyed that part.

Caren and I began talking every day, I would be excited to wake up and see her and she was always excited to see me. It just seemed to fit very well.

I found out she loved chocolate. And cupcakes. I decided to give her a big chocolate covered cupcake with 2 big cherries on top, and sprinkles.

9 months later and she still tells me that is what got to her. Although the cupcake may have finally reeled her in there is much more than that.

In these 9 months we have been together we have had many great times. Memorable moments filled with love. There's also been bad. We've had fights as all couples do.

And the worst is when she gets sick. Especially when she went into a coma. I didn't know how to feel or what to do then but no matter what I love this girl with all my heart.

I hope that long after this book is old falling apart we are still having great times together.

S